THE GHOST OF POPCORN HILL

3.5
Austin
Gomes

Other Little Apple Paperbacks
you will enjoy:

The Ghost of Windy Hill
by Clyde Robert Bulla

The Haunting of Grade Three
by Grace Maccarone

The Secret House
by Carol Beach York

The Trickster Ghost
by Ellen Showell

Witch in the House
by Ruth Chew

THE GHOST OF POPCORN HILL

BETTY REN WRIGHT

INTERIOR ILLUSTRATIONS BY KAREN RITZ

A
LITTLE APPLE
PAPERBACK

SCHOLASTIC INC.
New York Toronto London Auckland Sydney

ISBN 0-590-47873-7

12 11 10 9 8 7 6 5 4   4 5 6 7 8 9/9

Printed in the U.S.A.   40

First Scholastic printing, October 1994

FOR
Lauren and Courtney

Contents

THE GHOST OF POPCORN HILL

CHAPTER ONE

"Ho-Ho-Ho!"

"Ho-ho-ho!"

"Stop laughing," Martin said. He glared across the dark room at his little brother's bed.

"I'm not laughing," Peter protested. "I thought that was you."

"Well, it wasn't." They listened for a while, and then Martin went on with his story. "So Jimmy Adams couldn't find his kitten, and everybody thought it was dead or something."

Peter moved restlessly under his covers.

3

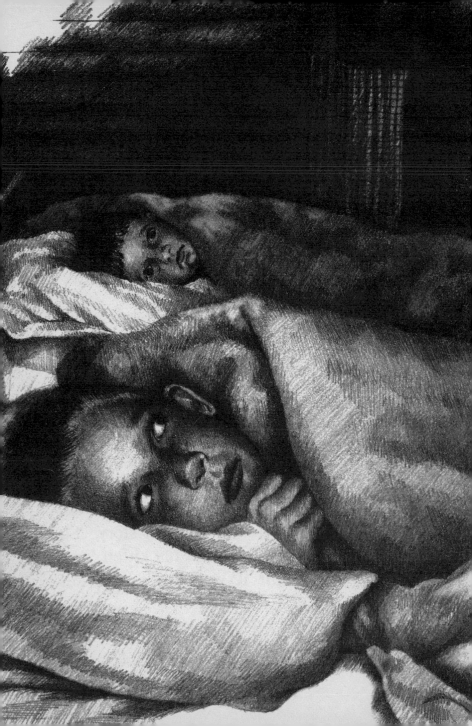

"I don't like this story," he said. "It's too sad."

"No it's not," Martin said. "Because they found the kitten finally, and do you know where he was?"

"How would I know that?"

"He was in the salad bowl, in the kitchen sink. All covered with French dressing and sound asleep." Martin chuckled to himself, and then he stopped again to listen. "You did laugh before," he said. "During the sad part."

"Didn't."

"Did."

Both boys lay very still, and Martin discovered he had goose bumps. He knew he had heard a laugh.

"I'm scared," Peter whispered, sounding as if he might cry.

Martin took a deep breath. "Forget about who laughed," he ordered. "Think about something nice. Think about tomorrow when we get the dog."

Peter stopped sniffling. "It'll be the biggest dog in the whole world," he murmured in a dreamy voice. "I can't wait."

"So go to sleep," Martin said. "Tomorrow will come faster."

A minute or two later, soft snores told him Peter had taken his advice. That was the trouble with being three years older. You had to stay awake and do all the worrying. Now that he'd started thinking about the dog they were going to get tomorrow, he had to worry about *that*. Would it really be the biggest dog in the world? That was what both boys wanted. A big dog could pull their wagon around the yard. In the wintertime he could drag their sled up Popcorn Hill. He would be the perfect pet, but Martin wasn't at all sure they were going to get him.

The trouble was their father. He insisted that a big dog wouldn't fit in their little old cabin. A big dog would cost too much to feed. *Remember, we moved to Popcorn Hill when I lost my job, and we have to save some money,* he'd told Martin and Peter about a hundred times in the last few months. *Let's be sensible about this.*

"I don't want to be sensible," Martin whispered unhappily into the darkness. "I want a big dog as much as Peter does."

And then, to his horror, it happened again. *"Ho-ho-ho,"* something laughed. *"Ho-ho-ho-ho-ho!"*

It was the scariest sound Martin had ever heard.

CHAPTER TWO

Dog Day

Peter woke up first.

"Today's the day," he shouted in Martin's ear. "Wake up, wake up, wake up!"

Martin yawned and pushed back the covers. The boys dressed quickly and went out to the kitchen, where their mother was making oatmeal for breakfast.

"You're up bright and early," she said cheerfully. "I bet I know why."

"It's dog day," Peter explained, as if he were the only one who kept track. Martin and his mother grinned at each other.

"It certainly is," Mrs. Tracy said. "I'm as excited as you are."

"No, I'm the most excited," Peter said. "I'm the most excited person in this house."

Martin opened the screen door and went outside. The cabin was small—one long room that was both kitchen and living room, and two bedrooms. The bathroom was a little house at the end of the yard, and the water they needed came from a pump next to the porch. *It isn't much of a place*, Martin's father had said when they moved in. *But it will have to do for now. And look at that view!*

Martin looked at the view every morning. From the top of Popcorn Hill you could see for miles. Fruit trees, with blossoms that looked like popcorn, dotted the hillside. Beyond were meadows and a creek, and there were woods everywhere. Maybe the cabin wasn't much of a house, but Martin knew he'd rather live there than anywhere else in the world.

When he went back inside, his father was

sitting at the round table. "Eat your breakfast, guys," he said. "We've got a job to do." He winked at Peter, and Peter blinked back.

Martin poured milk on his oatmeal and added some cinnamon. He wasn't hungry, but he knew he had to eat or his mother would think he was sick. There was so much to think about. The dog—the *big* dog. And the ghostly laughter they had heard last night. Should he tell his parents about that? He wanted to, but his father would probably make a joke about it, and his mother would think it was a burglar.

It wasn't a burglar, he assured her silently. *Burglars don't laugh like that. Nothing laughs like that.*

"Martin, you look worried," his father said. "Has the President of the United States been pestering you for advice again?"

Martin tried to smile. "Something weird happened last night," he mumbled. "We heard a man laughing."

His father took a sip of coffee. "Me," he said. "I laugh a lot. It's better than crying."

"It wasn't you, Daddy," Peter said. "This was really scary."

"Oh, dear, I hope it wasn't burglars!" Mrs. Tracy exclaimed. "I've been afraid of this. Living way out here, so far from every-body. . . ."

Mr. Tracy pushed back his chair. "It wasn't burglars. We don't have anything worth stealing," he said. "Anyway, after to-day you won't have to give burglars a thought. We'll have a dog to protect us." He grinned at Martin and Peter. "Ready to go? Last one in the truck is a leadfoot."

Martin was the last one in the truck, be-cause he didn't even run. He was too busy wishing he hadn't mentioned that mysteri-ous *Ho-ho-ho*. He didn't want his mother to think there was anything bad about living on Popcorn Hill. He wanted to live there for-ever.

CHAPTER THREE

Rosie

When they parked in front of the Humane Society, Martin felt as if it were Christmas and his birthday rolled into one. Too excited to talk, he and Peter followed their father into the office and then through another door. Big barks and little ones greeted them.

"Right this way," the caretaker said. "The dogs are on this aisle, and the cats are on the next one."

"We want a dog," Peter said. "A great big one."

Mr. Tracy shook his head. "Not a big one," he said firmly. "We just want a nice dog that'll be fun to have around the house."

"Gotcha," the caretaker said. He pointed at a tiny gray dog with long ears and a short, stand-up tail. "There's a lively little guy."

The gray dog yipped and jumped against the wire netting. Martin bit his lip. He felt sorry for the little dog, but he didn't want to take him home.

"I think maybe he's a bit *too* small," Mr. Tracy said. "What do you think, boys?"

Martin nodded. Peter had already moved to the next pen. His eyes were as round as marbles.

"Daddy, here he is!" he shouted. "Here's our dog!"

They gathered behind Peter and stared into the cage. A silver-coated German shepherd stared back at them.

"Oh, wow," Martin breathed. "He's perfect." He could picture the huge dog pulling their wagon and walking with them to school. Everyone would want to pet him, but they wouldn't dare until Martin or Peter said it was all right.

"He's *not* perfect," Mr. Tracy said. "And don't try to gang up on me, because it won't do any good. We don't have room for a dog this size. And we certainly can't afford to feed him." He was smiling, but there was a note in his voice that warned the boys not to argue.

They walked on, past a little brown-and-white spotted dog with a twisty tail, and a long, low mop of a dog that lay fast asleep.

"Next one's part Labrador," the caretaker said. "A real beauty!"

"Wow!" Peter breathed. The gleaming black dog was as big as a pony.

"Don't even ask," Mr. Tracy said.

The caretaker patted Peter's head. "Wait'll you see what we have in the last pen," he said cheerfully. "You'll love her."

The dog in the last pen was black too, with lots of white patches. Her feathery tail swept back and forth, and she pressed her freckled nose against the netting.

"She's a honey," the caretaker told them. He looked from Martin to Peter. "She's only about ten months old—just right for training." Then he turned to Mr. Tracy. "Won't get much bigger than she is right now."

Nobody spoke. The caretaker opened the door and let the dog out into the aisle. She danced around Martin and Peter with excited little barks.

"What do you say, boys?" their father asked. "She looks as if she'd be happy to join the family."

Martin and Peter crouched. The dog licked their faces. Then she sat in front of them and cocked her head.

"I call her Rosie," the caretaker said. "My daughter Rose has freckles like that. Of course, you could call her anything you wanted."

Martin and Peter and Rosie looked at each other. *She's a nice enough little dog,* Martin thought. He knew Peter was thinking the same thing. And if they didn't take this dog, they weren't going to get one.

16

"Hey, Rosie," Martin said. "Do you want a ride in a truck?"

Rosie leaped into the air like a missile. She jumped on Martin and then on Peter, knocking him over. Her body trembled with excitement.

"I think you've got a dog," the caretaker said with a grin. He led the way back to the office, and the Tracys followed with Rosie bouncing beside them.

"Good girl," Martin told her. She really was a nice dog. He and Peter took turns petting her as they walked. They were careful not to look into the pens where the black Labrador and the silver German shepherd were still waiting for someone to claim them.

CHAPTER FOUR

A Surprise Visitor

Mrs. Tracy loved Rosie the minute she saw her. She gave the boys her old bathrobe to make a cozy bed next to the stove.

"I'll feel so much better having a dog in the house," she said. "In case those prowlers come back again."

That afternoon Martin and Peter tied a rope to Rosie's collar and took her for a walk around the hilltop. She sniffed every tree and peered under bushes, but mostly she ran along next to the boys and jumped on them.

"She likes us," Martin said.

Peter didn't answer.

"We can teach her lots of tricks," Martin added. "She's smart."

"That German shepherd dog was smarter," Peter said. "I could tell."

When they returned to the cabin, they rolled a ball back and forth across the kitchen for Rosie to chase.

"I'd say she's great at chasing and pretty terrible at bringing back," their father commented. He was getting ready to go to town again for his four-nights-a-week job at the supermarket.

"She's good at chewing, too." Mrs. Tracy held up a letter that had fallen on the floor. It was ripped almost in two. "We'll have to be careful."

After supper the boys carried a bag of garbage out to the pit at the end of the lot. Then they sat on a big rock and looked down at the apple orchard at the foot of the hill. Beyond it they could see the roof of the old deserted mill, and beyond that a little of the creek that

wound around Popcorn Hill. The air was soft as silk.

"What's that?" Martin asked suddenly. Something was moving among the apple trees.

Peter grabbed his arm.

"It could be a deer," Martin whispered.

"Maybe it's a wolf." Peter slid off the rock. "Come on, Martin, let's go."

"That's crazy," Martin said. But he stood up too, just in case.

A moment later both boys gasped in surprise. A shaggy gray-and-white Old English sheepdog trotted out from under the trees and looked around. Even from this distance they could see that he was *big*.

Peter was the first to speak. "He's lost," he said positively. "He needs friends. Come *on*, Martin."

Together the boys hurried along the path that led down the hillside. There was something thrilling about the way the huge sheepdog stood there waiting. He seemed to be inviting them to join him.

But when they reached the bottom of the hill and Peter called, "Here, boy!" the dog darted away. He ran along the edge of the orchard, then doubled back and stopped.

"Come on, boy." Martin held out his hand. This time the dog raced right past them, long hair flying. The boys started to follow, but the dog turned and darted in among the trees. He looked over his shoulder once, and Peter gave a crow of delight.

"He smiled at us!" he shouted. "Did you see!"

"Dogs don't smile," Martin said. He pulled Peter to a stop. It was getting dark, and they could no longer see the sheepdog. Suddenly the orchard seemed lonely and the cabin a long way off.

"We'd better go back," said Martin. "Mom will be worried."

All the way up the hill, Peter kept talking about the sheepdog. "If he's lost, he needs a place to live," he said. "That poor dog is all by himself."

"We have a dog," Martin reminded him.

But he kept remembering how hopefully the sheepdog had looked at them.

"He could pull the wagon," Peter said dreamily. "He's so big, he could pull *two* wagons. I really liked him."

So did I, thought Martin. Ahead of them, the lights of the cabin twinkled in the dark. Martin walked faster. "I'm going to teach Rosie to sit tonight," he said. "It'll be her first lesson."

"That sheepdog knows lots of tricks already," Peter said. "I can tell."

CHAPTER FIVE

"Who's Going to Believe Us?"

"Oh, no!"

It was just before lunch the next day. Mrs. Tracy stood in the middle of the kitchen, a shredded dish towel in one hand and a badly chewed scrubbing brush in the other. "Bad girl!" she scolded.

"Bad girl!" Peter echoed.

Rosie flattened herself on the floor. Her tail swept back and forth across the linoleum, and her brown eyes were pleading.

"She didn't mean to hurt anything, Mom," Martin said. "See how sorry she is?"

Rosie crossed her paws in front of her and looked so worried that Mrs. Tracy laughed in spite of herself.

"She's telling you it won't happen again," Martin said.

But he was wrong. That same afternoon he found one of his brand-new sneakers chewed almost in two. This time he didn't laugh. He'd waited a long time for those sneakers.

"I bet that sheepdog wouldn't chew things," Peter said in bed that night. He'd spent a good part of the day looking down at the orchard. "I wish he was our dog. Rosie is lots of trouble."

Before Martin could answer, it happened. *"Ho-ho-ho!"*

Peter gave a squeal of terror. Martin leaped out of bed and raced out into the kitchen.

"Dad! Mom!" His legs flew out from under him as Rosie hurtled to meet him, filling the air with her barks. They rolled across the floor, ending up at the open door to Mr. and Mrs. Tracy's bedroom.

Martin's father switched on a light and blinked down at Martin. "What in the world—"

"In there," Martin gasped, pointing at his bedroom. "Someone's in there."

Mr. Tracy dashed into the bedroom, with Martin, his mother, and Rosie close behind him.

"Peter!" Mrs. Tracy shrieked. "Where's Peter?"

"I'm here," Peter said shakily. He pushed back the sheet that was covering his head and looked fearfully into the far corner of the room.

"Someone was over there in the corner, Dad," Martin said. "We both heard him. He was laughing."

"He was *what*?" Mr. Tracy sounded as if he couldn't believe he'd heard right.

"He was laughing," Martin repeated. But he was a little uncertain now. There was no one in the room and no place to hide.

His father rubbed his forehead. "Well, I'm *not* laughing," he said tiredly. "One of you is having a bad dream and scaring the other. Let's not have any more of that, okay?"

Martin swallowed hard. He climbed back into bed, and Mrs. Tracy kissed both boys good night. "I don't think it could have been a burglar," she said comfortingly. "Rosie would have heard him."

As soon as they were alone, Peter jumped out of his bed and climbed in with Martin. "I heard him," he sniffled. "I did!"

"So did I," Martin said. "But who's going to believe us? Nobody, that's who!"

CHAPTER SIX

The *Ho-Ho* Ghost

"I'm scared of ghosts," Peter said. "Specially ones that laugh." They were making their way down the path to the apple orchard.

Martin sighed. "Don't talk about it to anyone else," he warned. "Dad won't believe us, and Mom is still worried about burglars, even though she says she isn't. I saw her looking for footprints outside our bedroom window this morning."

"If we had a sheepdog, that ghost wouldn't

come around," Peter said. "He'd be too scared to."

They had been wandering through the orchard for nearly an hour when suddenly the dog appeared. Once again he watched them for a moment, then ran away when they called to him. Martin and Peter chased him, but he was very fast.

"Let's start back," Martin panted at last. "Maybe he'll follow us."

To their delight, that was what happened. The sheepdog stayed about fifty feet behind them all the way to the top of the hill. Then Rosie began to bark inside the cabin. The big dog turned and ran back down the path.

"That dumb Rosie!" Peter grumbled. "What good is she?"

When they went inside, they found that their mother was angry with Rosie too. Rosie had pulled a library book off a chair and had chewed the cover.

"If you'd take her outside with you, she wouldn't have so much time to get into trouble," Mrs. Tracy complained.

The boys looked at each other. They were pretty sure that if Rosie tagged along, the sheepdog would stay out of sight.

Every day after that the boys went down to the orchard. Twice the sheepdog came back, and each time he followed them up the hill before he ran away again.

"What are we going to do if we get him all the way to the house?" Martin wondered one night after the boys had gone to bed. "Mom and Dad will never let us keep him."

"Yes they will." Peter sounded sure. "When they see how nice he is, they'll have to."

"I don't think so . . ." Martin began sadly. Then he stopped.

"Ho-ho-ho!" came a laugh out of the darkness.

For a moment both boys were too startled to speak. Then Peter began to cry.

"Martin!" he whimpered. But Martin couldn't move. All he could do was cower under the covers as the laughter came again and again.

"Ho-ho-ho!"

Whoever it was, was right there in the bedroom.

CHAPTER SEVEN

The Loneliest Feller

"Martin, d-do something!" Peter's voice sounded muffled, as if his hands were covering his face. "M-make it go away!"

Martin took a deep breath. He stuck one foot out from under the covers and then the other. If he could just cross the room to the light switch . . . But before he could take a single step, a strange glow appeared in the corner. As he stared, the glow grew brighter and a tall, skinny figure began to take shape. Moonlight shone right through the mournful face, the raggedy trousers held up with

35

red suspenders, and the tattered shirt. He looked like a ghostly scarecrow.

"Martin!" Peter wailed and started to tumble out of bed.

"Don't fuss, boy," the ghost said in a hollow voice that was almost a moan. "No need to be afraid of old Tom Buffle."

Martin clutched his pillow as if it were a rubber raft that would save him from drowning. "Who are you? Wh-what do you want?"

The ghost shimmered and shook. "Tom Buffle's the name," he repeated. "Used to live in this cabin, I did. A long time ago. Right now I'm the loneliest feller you ever seed."

Peter scooted across the floor and dived into Martin's bed. He pulled the sheet over his head. "Go away!" he begged.

Tom Buffle's face grew sadder. "I just came by for a little chat," he moaned. "Thought we might be friends, like."

Martin shuddered. He couldn't imagine having a friend he was able to see through.

"Wh-why do you laugh like that?" he demanded. His voice shot up.

37

Tom Buffle shimmered wildly. "Just tryin' to be friendly," he groaned. "That's my way. Thought if I cheered you up, you'd let me come back every night."

At that, Peter started to cry so loudly that Martin was afraid his parents would hear.

"You'd better go," Martin said. "If my dad sees you, he'll be mad."

"Can't see me or hear me," Tom Buffle said, but he started to fade as Peter's sobs continued. "People and dogs can't hear me or see me less'n I let 'em." The last words came from a great distance. The corner was empty.

"He's gone," Martin whispered. "Hush up, Peter."

"Can't," Peter sobbed. He pushed back the sheet and looked around fearfully. "I don't want him to come back," he sniffled. "Not *ever!*"

Martin's hands were clammy. "What am I supposed to do about it?" he asked. "Besides, I feel kind of sorry for him. He says he's lonesome. And if he wants to come to talk to us, who's going to stop him?"

Somehow, though, he knew they had to find a way. Popcorn Hill was the best place in the world, but he could never get used to having a ghost shimmering in their bedroom.

The next morning Peter was white-faced and quiet. Martin wondered if he looked that scared himself. Surely someone would notice.

But he needn't have worried. Before they were dressed, there was a crash in the kitchen. They ran out to find Rosie hiding under the table and their mother looking at unbaked cookies scattered over the floor.

"She jumped up and pulled the cookie sheet off the table!" Mrs. Tracy exclaimed. "What are we going to do about that dog?"

Rosie stuck her nose out from under the table and nibbled a piece of cookie dough.

"If you boys paid more attention to her, maybe she'd behave better," Mrs. Tracy said crossly. "I don't understand—you wanted a dog so much, and now you hardly play with her. If we didn't need a watchdog, there'd be no reason to keep her."

Peter made a face, and Martin knew what he was thinking. *Some watchdog!*

The freckled nose came out again. Martin pushed another piece of cookie dough to where she could reach it. He sighed. Rosie was one problem and Tom Buffle was another—a big one! The only good things happening these days were the visits of the sheepdog. That sheepdog was the greatest dog a boy could ever have.

CHAPTER EIGHT

Lost!

"See you in the morning, gang." Mr. Tracy waved to the boys as the truck jolted down the hillside.

"I wish Daddy didn't have to go to work," Peter said uneasily. "I wish he could stay home."

"Let's look for the sheepdog," Martin suggested. "It won't be dark for a while." *And we won't have to think about Tom Buffle.*

They had barely sat down on their favorite rock when the big dog ambled out of the orchard. He looked up at the boys and began to run in circles at the foot of the hill.

"What's he doing?" Peter wondered.

Martin frowned. "I think he's doing what sheepdogs do when they're working," he said. "They run in circles and round up the sheep. Only he doesn't have any sheep."

"He could have us," Peter said suddenly. "We could let him round us up, and maybe we'd get close enough to pet him."

They ran down the hill, but as soon as they reached the bottom, the sheepdog darted back into the orchard. He waited for them to follow, then dashed away again.

"He doesn't want to play roundup," Peter said.

"But he wants us to come with him," Martin said. "And he's letting us get closer. Let's go!"

They dashed back and forth through the orchard after the dog. Sometimes the sheepdog let them come quite close before he ran away. Then, without warning, he was gone, racing into the woods beyond the orchard.

"He'll be back," Martin said. "He really wants us to catch him."

"What's that?" Peter stopped short at the edge of a clearing. A building loomed in the half dark.

"It's the old mill," Martin said. "Nobody's lived there for a million years." He grabbed Peter's hand and pulled him back into the woods. The deserted mill was frightening, and besides, Martin was suddenly aware of how late it was. "We'd better go home," he said.

They started walking, first in one direction, then in another. Martin stumbled over a root and fell flat, dragging his little brother down beside him.

"I'm going to climb a tree and look for Popcorn Hill," he said. "You stay right here."

Climbing was hard, especially in the dark. "There are lots of hills," he told Peter when he came back down. "I can't tell which one is ours. We'll just have to wait. Mom will call

Dad when we don't come home, and they'll find us."

"That'll take a long time," Peter sniffled. "I'm scared, Martin."

Martin was scared too, but he didn't want to say so. They curled up with their backs against a tree trunk and waited. Something swooshed overhead.

"Just a bat," Martin said, trying to sound calm.

"Look!" Peter shrieked a few minutes later. He pointed at a pair of yellow eyes gleaming in the dark. "There's Tom Buffle!"

"No, it's not," Martin said hoarsely. "That's something little. A skunk maybe."

"Yuk!" Peter moved closer to Martin, but he stopped sniffling. A skunk wasn't as bad as a ghost.

A long time passed. Then they heard something Martin couldn't explain. It was a rustling sound, far off at first but getting closer fast.

"A wolf's coming to get us," Peter wailed. "What'll we do?"

"It's not a wolf," Martin quavered. "It's nothing." But the next moment he gave a yelp of terror. The "nothing" was right there in the clearing, panting in his ear and jumping all over him.

CHAPTER NINE

The Ghost Again!

"It's Rosie!"

Martin couldn't see the nose full of freckles or the long red tongue that was licking his face, but he knew. Rosie had come to rescue them.

"Is it really?" Peter quivered. A feathery tail swept across his face. "Hey, it is!"

"Take us home, Rosie," Martin ordered. He scrambled to his feet and waited anxiously. Rosie had found them, but would she know the way back? She had never been this far from the cabin before.

Rosie knew. She set off at once, stopping every few feet to make sure the boys were following. At first it was hard to keep track of her in the dark, but after a few minutes of stumbling and bumping into Peter, Martin discovered they were walking between long rows of trees in the apple orchard.

"Good dog!" Martin shouted.

"Martin! Peter!"

"It's Mom!" Martin grabbed Peter's hand and pulled him along. "Look, there's our hill."

They raced up the path, never stopping till they reached the top of Popcorn Hill, where their mother was waiting.

"Thank goodness!" she exclaimed. She hugged them both, while Rosie danced around them. "Whatever made you wander off like that?" she scolded. "I couldn't think what to do but let Rosie out to see if she could find you."

"We didn't notice how dark it was getting," Martin said. He hadn't answered his mother's question, but he hoped she

wouldn't ask it again. He hated to admit they'd been chasing a dog, when they had Rosie waiting for them at home.

"You should have told Mom about the sheepdog," Peter said later, when they were in bed. "She would feel sorry for him out there all by himself. Maybe she'd tell Daddy we need two dogs."

"I don't think so," Martin said. "We're lucky to have one. Besides, the sheepdog ran off and left us, and Rosie brought us home. Rosie is a pretty neat dog."

Peter sighed. "Just the same," he said, "I wish—"

"*Ho-ho-ho!*" There was a glimmering in the corner, and a touch of red that could have been suspenders.

"No, *no!*" Peter gasped. "Go away!"

"Just came for a chat," said the hollow voice. "Thought we could talk about things, friendly like."

Martin gulped. He knew Tom Buffle was lonely, but he also knew Peter was getting ready to cry. "I— I'm sorry," he stammered.

"We can't talk now. We're— we're sort of tired." It was the only excuse he could think of, and he realized it sounded made-up.

Tom Buffle sighed. "Everyone can use a friendly chat once in a while," he moaned. "Especially me." But his voice faded away to nothing as he spoke, and then the corner of the room was dark once more.

Martin felt terrible.

CHAPTER TEN

"It Can't Happen"

"You're both grounded for a week," Mr. Tracy announced the next morning. "You know you gave your mother a bad scare last night."

Martin stared in dismay. Peter's lower lip trembled. "Daddy—"

"No whining," their father said firmly. "There's plenty of room to play up here on the hill."

Peter ran outside. Martin followed more slowly, with Rosie at his heels. They sat on the rock at the end of the lot while Rosie wandered around, exploring.

"Now we'll never catch the sheepdog," Peter said mournfully. "And he was starting to let us get close!"

Just then the big dog trotted out of the orchard and looked up.

"If we don't go down, he'll run away and find some other kids to live with," Peter said. "What're we going to do, Martin?"

"We can't do anything," Martin said. "We're stuck."

For the next week they went regularly to look down at the orchard. Sometimes the sheepdog was waiting for them. Sometimes he didn't appear at all.

"He's going to give up," Peter said gloomily. "He's going to go away, and we'll never see him again."

Martin wished he could make his brother feel better. "At least Tom Buffle hasn't come around for a while," he reminded Peter.

"He has too," Peter argued. "He started to

come night before last—I saw his suspenders and a little bit of his shirt. If I hadn't cried, he would have been *ho-ho-ho*ing all over the place."

Martin was sorry he'd brought up Tom Buffle. He felt bad every time he thought about the poor, lonely ghost.

"Well, at least Rosie isn't chewing stuff anymore," he said, to change the subject. During the days they'd been grounded, he had taught Rosie to roll over and to sit up and beg.

Peter was silent. He didn't care what Rosie did.

When the last night of the grounding finally came, the boys couldn't sleep. Tomorrow they would be able to go down to the orchard again.

Suddenly Peter sat up in bed. "What's that noise?" he asked, looking around uneasily.

Martin heard it too—a soft *scritch-scratch* at the screen. He slipped out of bed and tiptoed to the window. Peter followed him.

They stared into the moonlit yard, not daring to believe their eyes.

"It's him!" Peter exclaimed joyfully. "He came to find us."

The sheepdog stood just outside the window, looking at them. Trembling with excitement, Martin opened the screen and stepped back.

"Come, boy," he whispered. And the sheepdog came, leaping through the window. He ambled around the bedroom, sniffing the beds and poking his huge head into corners.

"I'm going to pet him," Peter whispered. "Watch."

He took a step forward and stopped. "Martin?" His voice rose in a wail.

Martin felt a lurch in the pit of his stomach. He blinked and looked again to see if the sheepdog was really glimmering and shimmering.

It was true. The moonlight was shining right through him!

"It Can't Happen"

"It can't happen," Peter sobbed. "A dog can't be a ghost!"

Martin was as disappointed as he was frightened. "This one is," he said grimly. "We just never got close enough to notice before."

The sheepdog looked from one of them to the other, as if he were wondering what the fuss was about. Then he leaped up and floated across the room and out the window.

CHAPTER ELEVEN

"Good Girl!"

"I suppose you two will be off and running this morning," Mr. Tracy said at breakfast. "Has it been a long week?"

"Sort of," Martin said. Until last night it had seemed like the longest week of his life. Now it didn't matter. Now he knew the sheepdog could never join their family.

"What do *you* say, Peter?" their father asked curiously.

"Nothing." Peter didn't look up. He made a hole in the middle of his oatmeal and watched it fill with milk.

Mr. Tracy leaned over and gave Rosie a pat. "Couple of grumps we have here this morning," he said. "You keep an eye on them today, Rosie. Don't let them get lost."

"Are you coming home for lunch, or do you want to take some sandwiches with you?" their mother asked.

"Sandwiches," Martin said. He caught his father's eye and added, "Please." For the first time since they'd moved there, he was eager to get away from Popcorn Hill for a while.

Without even discussing it, the boys headed down the road in front of the cabin and away from the orchard. Rosie romped around them, chasing butterflies and sassing the squirrels that chattered in the trees.

"She's silly," Peter said. He kicked a stone into the brush at the side of the road.

"She's happy," Martin said. But Rosie's cheerful mood was getting on his nerves. In spite of the shining day, all he could think about was ghosts. Now there were two of them haunting Popcorn Hill, and one of them was the dog he and Peter had dreamed of owning.

"Want to go to the creek?" Martin asked.

Peter shrugged. "Okay. I guess."

By the time they reached the creek, they were tired and hot. The water was only about a foot deep, but it ran swiftly over the rocky bottom, making a cool *plish-plash*. The boys sat on the bank and took off their sneakers. Rosie barked at the ripples.

"She's never seen a creek before," Martin said. "Wonder what she thinks it's for."

A moment later Rosie showed them she knew. With a happy bark she leaped into the middle of the stream. Back and forth she splashed, sometimes jumping, sometimes swimming. When she spotted a big stone halfway across, she scrambled up onto it and barked at the boys.

"She looks funny," Peter said, almost smiling. Rosie's coat was plastered to her thin body, and her feathery tail whipped the air like a wet rope.

"She wants us out there with her," Martin said. "Come on."

They splashed toward the rock, with Rosie getting more excited every second. When Martin was just a couple of feet away, she launched herself into the air, hitting him squarely on the chest. Down he went, knocking over Peter on the way. They crouched in the water and watched Rosie climb back on the rock.

"It's a game!" Martin laughed. "She's made up a game. She wants to defend that rock. She doesn't want us near it."

"You stay here and I'll go around to the other side," Peter said, splashing noisily through the water. "She won't know what to do."

But Rosie was ready for him. For the next twenty minutes she defended herself against every attack, hurtling at them like a black-and-white cannonball when they got too close. Again and again the boys toppled backward, partly because it pleased Rosie so much and partly because the water felt good.

61

"Good Girl!"

When they were too tired to play the game anymore, they waded to shore and opened the lunch bag their mother had packed. Rosie barked at them to come back, but soon she gave up too and joined them.

Peter broke off a corner of his peanut butter sandwich and dropped it in front of her.

"Good girl!" he said softly.

After lunch they followed the creek bed for a while, watching for fish and throwing stones in the water. Then they turned back toward home.

"I've got an idea," Martin said slowly. "I've been thinking about—well, you know." He hated to say the words and possibly spoil the day.

"What?" Peter looked at him suspiciously.

"About having two ghosts."

"Don't talk about it," Peter ordered.

"We have to," Martin said. "They're there, aren't they? Tom Buffle's hanging around because he's lonesome, and the sheepdog came last night because he wants friends too. What I was thinking is, why don't we try to get them together? If they have each other, they won't need us."

Peter stared. "How could we do that?"

"I'm not sure," Martin said. "We'd have to wait till the dog came back again, and then we'd have to figure out a way to make Tom Buffle appear at the same time."

Peter's eyes widened in horror. "No, no, *no!*" he roared. "You can't! You mustn't!" Rosie dashed between them, barking wildly.

"We have to," Martin said. It seemed to him that a shadow had settled over them, even though there wasn't a cloud in the sky. "We can't lie awake watching for ghosts every night, can we?" He paused. "Can we?"

"Don't talk about it," Peter said.

CHAPTER TWELVE

"If He Does Come Again, We'll Be Ready"

"Let's go out to the rock and watch for the ghost dog," Martin whispered after supper that night. "If he sees us looking, maybe he'll come back to the cabin tonight."

Peter shook his head. He picked up a ball from the bedroom floor and rolled it out into the kitchen for Rosie to chase. "I'd rather play with Rosie," he said. "You'd better not go either."

But Martin was determined. Now that he'd thought of bringing Tom Buffle and the sheepdog together, he was going to find a way. It was the only answer he could think of to their problem.

It was lonely out on the rock without Peter. Fog rested like cotton candy over the tops of the trees in the valley. Martin sat down and wrapped his arms around his knees.

If I see the dog, I'll just wave at him and run back to the cabin, he decided uneasily. He didn't like ghosts any more than Peter did.

Minutes dragged by while he sat and thought about the ghost dog and Tom Buffle. Below him, the orchard and the little meadow in front of it disappeared from sight. The fog began creeping up Popcorn Hill.

Martin shivered. Bit by bit, the path up the hill vanished. *The dog could be right here before I know it,* he thought. He listened hard and imagined he heard the soft *flip-flop* of big paws.

He's here! Martin jumped down off the rock and raced headlong toward the

lights of the cabin. He had hoped to make sure the sheepdog was still around, but he didn't want to meet him out here all alone.

Mrs. Tracy was reading and Peter was drawing a picture when Martin burst through the doorway. Peter followed him into the bedroom.

"Did you see him?"

Martin peered out into the mist-filled yard. There was no sign of the dog. "I didn't see him," he admitted. "But I'm pretty sure he was close by. And I've thought of a plan. If he does come again, we'll be ready."

"I don't want to hear it," Peter said.

Martin made a face. He was scared himself, and his brother wasn't helping. "Don't you want to get rid of the ghosts?" he demanded.

Peter wouldn't look up. "Sure I do," he mumbled.

"Then you'd better listen, because you have to help."

Peter threw himself down on his bed.

"If He Does Come Again, We'll Be Ready"

"What do I have to do?" he asked unwillingly.

"Something you're real good at," Martin said. He was still annoyed. "You have to cry." And then he explained the plan he'd thought of, sitting out there in the fog.

CHAPTER THIRTEEN

How the Plan Worked

Mrs. Tracy was sleepy and decided to go to bed early. That made the first part of the plan easy. Just before the boys climbed into bed themselves, they lifted the screen out of the bedroom window.

"I know a ghost dog could come right through a screen if he wanted to, but we have to be sure he knows he's welcome," Martin explained.

"He's not welcome," Peter said stubbornly. "I wish Daddy were home. What if something goes wrong? I'm scared."

"There's nothing to worry about," Martin said. He was glad Peter couldn't see the goose bumps on his arms.

"I wish Rosie could come in and sleep with us," Peter persisted. "She'd like that."

Martin didn't answer. Peter knew very well why Rosie couldn't be with them. If she got excited and started jumping around, the ghost dog might not come.

The boys were still for a while, listening to the wind that had blown the fog away. Moonlight spilled through the window. Then the wind faded to a breeze, and Martin heard the same soft *flip-flop* steps he had heard earlier in the evening.

Something panted at the windowsill.

"Oh, no!" Peter whimpered. He crouched under the covers with just one eye showing as the sheepdog leaped through the window and landed in the middle of the bedroom.

Martin watched the big dog explore the room. Each time he passed the window, moonlight shone through him.

I don't know if I can do this! Martin

thought in a panic. One ghost was bad enough. Two would be even scarier. But then he remembered how sorry he'd felt for Tom Buffle. Tom wanted a friend, and the sheepdog wanted one too. Otherwise the dog wouldn't be here, pacing around their bedroom in the middle of the night.

He took a deep breath and started the next step of the plan. It was simple. He was going to tell a story, the saddest story he could think of. If he made it sad enough, Tom Buffle might come to cheer them up.

"Once upon a time," he began in a shaky voice, "two boys were left all alone in a cabin in the woods."

The sheepdog wandered over to Peter's bed and sniffed his pillow.

"Cry!" Martin whispered. "This is supposed to be a sad story." Then he realized he didn't have to tell his brother what to do. Peter was already crying, because of the dog, not because of the story.

Martin started again. "So these two boys—" He stopped. He couldn't think of what to say next! Usually when he told a story, he put in real adventures and made-up ones, and the ideas came faster than he could say the words. But not this time. The ghost dog and Peter's muffled sobs had dried up every thought in his head.

"So these two boys what?" Peter sniffled. The sheepdog ambled across the bedroom and rested his see-through head close to Martin's.

"I— I don't know," Martin groaned. His plan was falling apart, and all because he hadn't made up the story in advance.

The sheepdog padded to the window. He looked as if he might be going to jump out.

"So the poor boys didn't have anything to eat!"

Martin couldn't believe his ears. Peter had stopped crying. In a quivery, shivery voice, he was telling the next part of the story.

"It was snowing, and they didn't have any wood for the stove," Peter went on. He looked fearfully into the corner where Tom Buffle had stood in the past.

"And they didn't have any blankets. Not even a little one." There was another pause. Martin held his breath.

"They didn't have anything to play with, either." Peter began to sound desperate.

"They didn't have any games."

Was that a faint, far-off *"Ho-ho-ho"*? Martin wasn't sure.

"And no storybooks."

"Ho-ho-ho!" This time there could be no doubt.

"They didn't have a dog, either!" Peter's voice faded to a whimper as the scarecrow figure began to appear. First came the long, narrow face, then the red suspenders, then the ragged trouser legs. A booming *"HO-HO-HO!"* brought a quick end to Peter's story.

"I can't do it anymore," he wailed softly and disappeared again under the covers.

"That's a very sad story," the ghost moaned. "Let me cheer you up."

Martin had almost forgotten the ghost dog, but now a movement at the window caught his eye. The sheepdog had whirled around

and was staring into the corner. He seemed to hesitate, and then with a great bound he crossed the room and threw himself against Tom Buffle's chest.

For a moment the two ghosts disappeared entirely. Martin sank back on his pillow in despair. But then they returned, glimmering and shimmering more brightly than ever. Tom Buffle hugged the sheepdog as if he'd never let him go.

"Buster!" he shouted, and this time there wasn't a trace of a moan in his voice. "Buster, is it really you?"

CHAPTER FOURTEEN

"A Great Dog!"

"Buster," Martin repeated. "Is that his name?"

"Sure is." The sheepdog put his paws on Tom Buffle's shoulders and licked his face.

"Is he— was he— your dog?" Peter asked, forgetting to be scared.

"Nope." Tom Buffle gave the dog another hug. "This here old feller belonged to my best friend, Jim Curly. They lived in the mill on the other side of the orchard. Buster disappeared in a storm one night, and we figured he got swept away in the creek. And then Jim moved down south. Buster must have come back to the mill to look for his pal, and he couldn't find him."

The ghost dog wagged his tail.

"Wish I'd gone over to the mill to look around," Tom said with a groan. "We could have gotten together a long time ago. But there didn't seem any point to goin' there. When Jim Curly left, it just stood empty. Funny that I never ran into Buster up here."

"He only came here once before," Martin explained. "I think he's sort of shy. And I guess he'd rather be at the mill, anyway. He led us over there once."

Tom Buffle gave Buster a hug. "Poor old feller. He's lonesome, same as me—aren't you, boy?"

"That's what we figured," Martin said eagerly. "We thought you two ought to get together. We didn't know you were already friends."

"You mean you fellers planned this?" the ghost asked. "You wanted to cheer up old Tom Buffle?"

"And make you go away," Peter said honestly. "Because we don't need to be cheered up. And now that you have Buster, you won't need us."

If Tom Buffle's feelings were hurt, he didn't let it show. "That's 'bout the nicest thing anybody ever did for me," he said. "And it's goin' to make Buster pretty happy too, ain't it, old boy?"

Buster glanced over his shoulder and then went back to licking Tom Buffle's face.

"He smiled at us," Peter said. "Did you see, Martin?"

Martin started to say "Dogs don't smile," but changed his mind. Buster *had* smiled.

"We'll be on our way then," Tom Buffle said. "Maybe we'll settle in the old mill—if that's what Buster wants." The figures grew fainter as he spoke, and soon the corner was as dark as if they had never been there.

Martin drew a long breath. "It worked!" he exclaimed. "You were real good helping out with the story, Peter. You didn't even sound scared—much."

"I *was* scared though," Peter admitted. "But I wanted the ghosts to go away more than I wanted to hide."

The boys were silent, thinking over what had just happened. Martin got up and put the screen in the window. He was about to climb back into bed when there was a scratching at the door to the kitchen. He opened the door a crack, and Rosie pushed her way in. They watched as she circled the room and stood up on her hind legs to look out the window.

"You know what's nice about Rosie?" Peter said. "She's fun and she's smart."

"That's right," Martin said.

"And she loves us," Peter said.

"Right," Martin agreed.

"And you can't see through her," Peter said. "She's solid."

Rosie ran over to Martin's bed and jumped up on his stomach. "She's solid, all right," Martin gasped. "She's a great dog."

ABOUT THE AUTHOR

BETTY REN WRIGHT is the author of many popular books for young readers, including *The Dollhouse Murders*, which was a *Booklist* Editors' Choice, and *Christina's Ghost* and *Ghosts Beneath Our Feet*, which were both IRA-CBC Children's Choices. *The Ghost of Popcorn Hill* is her first early chapter book.

Ms. Wright, an enthusiastic grandmother, lives in Wisconsin with her husband, painter George Frederiksen, and their cat and dog.